Ben Delta

an untold story

a novel

by

Marie Garcia

Ben Delta   Marie Garcia

Acknowledgments

I just want to thank those of you who helped me go over this piece with a fine tooth comb. I also want to thank my co-workers for putting up with how often I said aloud how many words I had written and how many I had left to go. Thank you for encouraging me while I wrote this!

Ben Delta   Marie Garcia

Dedication

To my husband for letting me
complain about how things
were going. To my co-workers
for encouraging me. To Lilly for
telling me I was a rock star.

Ben Delta

Marie Garcia

Untold Stories

Haden Delta, Volume 1

Tessa Kellogg-Easter, Volume 1

Tessa Kellogg-Easter, Volume 2

Pagan

Ben Delta   Marie Garcia

Prologue

Vancouver, Washington

February 17, 2014

My older brother, Milo, was running around trying all of the windows in the house. He ran upstairs and was yelling at my other brother, Elliott to try the doors.

There was a white haze all over the house and it was making all of us cough. My sisters, Amethyst and Willow, were standing in the middle of the living room. Amethyst was holding me.

"What should we do?" Willow asked, coughing.

"We need to protect Ben, Willow," Amethyst said. "There's got to be a closest or something that might be spared."

Willow looked over to the coat closest that was near the kitchen. "There?"

"Good." Amethyst looked at me. "Ben, I hope you survive. You're a good boy. Remember that Mommy and Daddy love you. That me and Willow and Aria and Emerald and Tessa love you. That Elliott and Milo do, too."

I nodded. I knew that. She was scaring me.

Amethyst carried me tot he closest, opened the rood, and placed me inside before closing the door. I started crying.

"Where's Ben?" Elliott asked, voice muffled.

"In the closet," Willow replied. Her voice was muffled, too.

"Why?"

"He's only three years old, Elliott," Amethyst said, coughing. "We need to protect him."

"Who would do this?" Milo asked.

"I don't know. Are there any windows that will open? Doors?"

"No. Not even upstairs."

"Can they be broken?"

"No."

"We're going to die, aren't we?"

"Yes, I think so."

"Let's move a bit away from the closet. I don't want him to hear us."

I heard them move a little bit away and it downed like their voices were lower to the ground. It was getting hot in the closet and I laid down. I could see them huddled together.

I started crying.

I heard Amethyst try to comfort me. It took awhile, I'm not sure how long, but eventually they all got quiet.

* * *

The closet door opened and someone I didn't know gasped.

"Poor baby," the figure whispered. It sounded like a girl. "Such negligence. They don't deserve you."

I tried to look for my brothers and sisters, but it got dark.

"Be quiet, baby. I'm going to save you and take you somewhere safe. These people won't ever see you again. Just stay quiet, baby."

I felt warmth. Arms around my body. Rushing.

"Leaving, Linney?" a deep voice asked. It sounded like a boy. A man.

"Yeah, Chief," the softer voice replied. "The kids. Too much."

"Understood."

The rushing movement got faster. I heard a door open and close. A car start and then more moving.

Chapter One

Spokane, Washington
February 18, 2014

We pulled off the road very early the next morning. The person who pulled me away from my home had driven us to her home. She had left me in her car while she had gone into her house.

She was gone for a long time and when she came back it was with a couple of bags. She tossed them into the backseat.

We stopped two more times before we had driven for a very long time. I was hungry and tired and scared. I didn't now this person that I was with.

She seemed nice, but I wanted my Mommy and my Daddy. My brothers and sisters. My aunts. Uncles. Cousins. Grandma and Grandpa.

I started to cry.

"It's okay, baby," she said. "I'm your mommy. Your name is Brendan Hudson Sanders."

I shook my head, tears flying. "My name is Ben Delta," I said, tearfully.

"Not anymore."

"Please, take me home. I want my Mommy and Daddy!"

"Sweetie, they left you alone in a burning house."

I shook my head.

* * *

"Welcome to the Quality Inn Oakwood," the lady said. "Oh, is he okay?"

"Yes," the woman said, bouncing me. "We're running away from a bad situation. My husband was abusive."

"I'm sorry!"

"We just need a room for the night."

"Of course." The woman across from us handed the woman that was holding me something and we then we left her.

Chapter Two

February 21, 2014

Nampa, Idaho

"Brendon, we're finally home," my new mommy said.

I nodded.

She wasn't treating me badly. She fed me. She'd gotten me some new clothes and some new toys. Gave me a bath.

"We'll be safe here, baby."

"Okay," I said.

"You're a good boy. I'll keep you safe."

"Okay."

"I'm going to put you in your playpen while I get things put away."

"Okay. Can I play with my blocks?"

She smiled. "Sure."

I held my arms up and she picked me up and placed me in the playpen. "Blocks?"

She laughed and picked them up from the floor. "Here you go, sweetie."

My new mommy turned on the TV and my old mommy was there.

"How are you and your family holding up?" a male asked. I didn't know him. I'd seen him on TV before though.

"We are devastated," Mommy said, crying. "We lost nearly all of our children. Tessa, Emerald, and Sage are our only surviving children. We will mourn the loss of Ben, Elliott, Milo, Willow, Amethyst, and Aria Spencer for the rest of our lives."

I tilted my head to the side. Trying to remember if Aria was there. Aria wasn't even there! I thought. Someone had come and taken her away. Then there was a lot of noise outside.

"We found out that the fire was deliberately set," Daddy said. "My wife was on vacation and I'd gone into work. My wife is a very dedicated police detective. We suspect that someone from her cases set it."

New mommy had come into the room and gasped.

"After the services, we will be going out of town while the debris is removed and the home rebuilt."

"If your children were still here, what would you tell them?"

Mommy looked directly at the camera. "Benny, you were so gentle and kind. Loving. Precious to us. Amethyst, you were an amazing young woman. Brave. Talented. Willow, you were special. An individual. Milo, a perfect gentleman. Elliott, so handsome. Kind. Helpful. Aria Spencer, you were so loved. All of you were."

"Remember that we love you. Always and forever," Daddy said. "Thank you."

Mommy and Daddy went into some building followed by Tessa and Sage and Emerald.

Ben Delta   Marie Garcia

    My poor sisters.

    I started to cry.

Chapter Three

My new mommy rushed and shut off the TV. She fell down on the floor and started to cry herself.

"What have I done?" she asked. "What have I done?"

"Mommy?" I asked. "You okay?"

She started shaking.

"What have I done? What have I done?"

"Mommy?"

All she did was go into the other room and close the door. I was alone for a long time.

* * *

Eventually, she finally came back out.

"Ben?" she asked. "Honey?"

"Mommy?" I asked, groggily. I must have fallen asleep.

"I hope you can understand that I can't take you home."

"How come? I don't un'stand."

She picked me up and took me into the kitchen and placed me in the high chair that she'd bought for me.

"Do you know what the word 'kidnap' means?"

I nodded. I heard it a lot at home since my Mommy was a police detective. "Yes. Means you take a baby or kid that's not yours."

"Yes. Well, a person. It doesn't only apply to children."

"Okay."

"I really thought that your parents didn't care when I found you. You were locked in a closet in a burning house."

I shook my head. "My sister, Amethyst, put me there."

"Why?"

"To save me."

She was moving around the kitchen making food. Smelled like spaghetti. I loved spaghetti.

"Why didn't they try to save themselves, too?"

"Milo and Elliott ran all over the house trying to find a way out. They couldn't. I could hear them coughing and crying after I was put in the closet. It got really hot. It was hard to breath. I fell asleep for a little bit."

"Oh, baby. I would take you back, but I'd just get in trouble. I'm so sorry."

I just looked away.

Chapter Four

February 21, 2014

I woke up, coughing. It's difficult to breath, just like when I was in the closet at home. "Help! Mommy!" I called.

I heard her turn her lamp on. I heard her rush from her room. The light came on in my room.

"What's wrong?" she asked, concerned.

"It hurts to breath. Feels like when I was in the closet a little bit."

"Okay." She picked me up ad we rushed out the door after she picked up her purse. We got into the new car that she'd bought after getting rid of the other one we drove here in.

"Where are we going?"

"I'm taking you to the hospital."

She buckled me into my car seat and we rushed to the closet hospital. I was coughing the whole time. She kept looking in the mirror to make sure I was okay.

* * *

"What's your name, little guy?" the man asked. I wanted to tell him the truth. "I'm a doctor."

"Brendan," I gasped. I didn't tell him. I wouldn't with her standing nearby.

"What's wrong, buddy?"

"Can't…"

"My name is Linney Sanders," my mommy said. "We fled from my abusive husband. We're in hiding."

"Okay."

"Brendan woke up crying and coughing about twenty minutes ago. He's having a hard time breathing."

"Any idea why?"

"He was in a fire. Please, don't report it." She had tears in her eyes.

"Did you…"

"No. My husband. I was at work and came home. I saw the flames and my husband wasn't there. I went in and looked for Brendan. The second I found him, I left."

"Okay. I won't report it. This time."

"Thank you. Please, help him."

"We'll see what we can do."

"Thank you."

Chapter Five

The doctor looked at me. They took me to various rooms and I ran tests. He put a tube up my nose. I felt air coming out of it. I didn't feel much better.

"Just breath, Brendan," the doctor said. "The tube has special air that will help you."

"Okay."

He turned to my new mommy. "We're going to need to keep him for a few days. His oxygen levels are very low."

"Okay," she said.

"We'll monitor him closely, but he should be okay."

"Great. Can I stay with him? He's so young to be by himself."

"Only during visiting hours. He'll be safe here. I promise."

She nodded.

"We'll move him to a room soon. Make sure that he eats."

"Thank you."

"Of course. The nurse will be in soon to move him."

She nodded and he left.

* * *

Once the doctor left, mommy looked at me.

"You better not say anything, Ben," she said.

"Why not?" I replied. My breathing was a little better. "I…"

She grabbed my arms really tight and squeezed them even harder. "*Your name is Brendan Hudson Sanders. We are in hiding because of your abusive father.* I promise you; Ben, you will never see your family again."

"I…"

"I mean it." Her hands gripped me tighter. "I will kill you."

"But..."

"Keep your little trap shut. I will make your life hell. Do you understand."

"Yes. I un'stand." I kept nodding.

"Good."

She let me go and there was a knock on the door.

"Ready to go, little guy?" a nice lady asked. "I'm a nurse. Are you okay?"

I nodded. "Yes. A ride sounds fun."

"Good. What's your name?"

"Brendan."

"Last name?"

"Good. Let's go."

The nurse went around the bed. She moved things around. She raised the handles of the bed and then got behind the it and started pushing me out of the door.

Chapter Six

February 23, 2014

"It's been two day!" mommy exclaimed. "When can I take him home?"

"His oxygen levels are still low," the doctor said. "He may need an oxygen tent."

"Why?"

"Your son may not be able to breathe without it."

"Ugh!"

The doctor glared at her. While I'd been in here, they doctors and nurses kept asking me my name. I kept telling them that it was Brendan. They didn't believe me.

When they weren't asking me my name then my mommy was asking me what they asked me and what I told them. She made sure that I was telling them what she'd told me to say.

My arm had bruised.

"Fine."

The doctor left the room and she whirled around to face me.

"What did you tell them?" she demanded.

"Nothing, Mommy," I said. "They keep asking me my name and I tell them Brendan. When you grabbed me there was a bruise on my arm."

"Are you sure you didn't say anything?"

"Yes, Mommy. I wouldn't say anything."

"Good. Like I said, I will kill you. There will be no one to mourn you. Your family thinks that you're already dead."

"I know. I won't say anything. You can t'ust me. I promise."

"I better be able to."

"You can. My mommy always told me to be a good boy. That's what I'm doing."

"I don't want to hear anything more about that woman."

She was starting to scare me. "Okay. I won't say anything. Do you think the doctor will let me have some blocks?"

"We can ask."

"Thank you."

She hit a button on the bed and a few minutes later a nurse came into the room. "Yes?" she asked.

"Could he get some blocks or something to play with?"

"Sure. I'll be back as soon as I can."

"Thank you."

The nurse nodded and left.

Chapter Seven

September 13, 2016
Kona, Idaho

"Mommy?" I called.

"Yeah, baby?" she replied.

Mommy, Linney, came into my room. It had been a little over two years since we'd moved from Nampa to Kona.

"Look." I held out my backpack. "Janey asked me to her birthday party on Tuesday. Can I go?"

"Sure. We have to get her a birthday present."

"A card, too?"

She laughed. "Of course."

"Yay!"

Today was my birthday, my *real* birthday. I only remember because it was always just after my brother's and sister's started back to school. Linney and I never celebrate it today though.

I remember a few things about my old life. We celebrate my birthday in February. The day that she "rescued" me is the date we use for my birthday.

I pretend not to remember my past. If I do then she hits me. If I don't then she doesn't hit me.

* * *

I had a journal hidden that I'd started keeping since I learned to write. It held everything that she'd done to me in it.

Mommy had gone to the store and left me with the neighbor.

The older girl always watched me, but never really paid attention to me. She was always on her phone.

I was in my and I kept the door shut.

Linney was always leaving. She almost always gone for hours. I don't think that she was working, though. I think she just didn't want to be around me.

I opened my journal to a random page and started to read the undated entry.

It read:

Finally, I was able to leave the hospital.

They had kept me in there for five days. The doctors thought that I was being abused my Linney, because of the bruises they'd found on my arms.

I didn't tell them the truth.

I kept quiet.

Linney said she would kill me.

She scares me.

Chapter Eight

I turned the page to another undated entry.

It read:

The birthday party at Janey's was so much fun!

She had a bounce house, a pony, and a clown! Janey was really girlie. She liked princesses and princes. Kings and queens. I thought that she'd have a princess themed party.

I'm glad I was wrong.

Janey and I went up to her room. No one missed us. I gave her a kiss. She looked so pretty in her little summer dress.

She showed me her dolls.

I don't like dolls. I like trucks, but she was so sweet. So cute.

Janey told me that she liked dogs. Those were my favorites, too!

After we kissed again, we went back to the party.

I guess that Janey is my girlfriend now.

Another undated entry read:

I hate Janey!

I saw her kissing another boy a recess today! I went up to her and she laughed at me.

Jenny had told me it was a dare!

Another undated entry said:

Linney has a boyfriend.

I hid in her closet last night. They were naked.

He played with her breasts. She really liked that. She played with his thing and he really liked that.

They both screamed a lot.

I left the room when they went to the bathroom to take a shower.

* * *

My food arrived.

Linney had spent most of my wait time in the bathroom. I don't think she was feeling well.

I turned on the TV and a picture of my mother was on the news.

The report said:

"*Decorated homicide detective, Addyson Delta was recently fired,*" the news anchor said. "*She was then re-hired after the apparent suicides of former partner, Jesus Meyers and her brother-in-law, Pagan Delta.*"

"Uncle Pagan?" I whispered.

"*Apparently, each man left a suicide note that will not be released to the public. Their families have asked for privacy and understanding during this time. The police department has not released a statement on the suicide of Detective Meyers and we're not likely to get one either. We do hope to speak with his father the warden of the Walla Walla prison.*"

"*Tragic,*" her co-anchor said.

"*Yes, it is.*"

"*Any word as to why Detective Delta was fired?*"

"*No.*"

"Thank you. Now, the weather."

The door to the bathroom opened and Linney came back into the main room and sat down beside me.

Chapter Nine

Linney was with another boyfriend. She brought him over for dinner. He looked different from the one that she had been with yesterday.

"Hey, buddy," he said. "What's your name?"

He smelled bad. Like he'd drank rubbing alcohol.

"Brendan," I said, wrinkling my nose. "You smell bad."

He backhanded me. "You mouthy little punk!"

"Andrew!" Linney exclaimed. "Don't. Stop."

"Bitch!"

"Brendan, go to your room. Don't open the door."

I ran to my room. I could hear him smacking her. She was screaming.

Finally, after a few minutes, I heard the same type of screaming I'd heard while I was in the closet.

I found my journal and opened it.

The undated entry I found read:

I miss my Mommy and Daddy.

I miss feeling loved and wanted.

Linney hit me again.

All I had been doing was sitting in the living room playing a video game.

She said that she'd called me. I didn't hear her. I didn't even have the TV up very loud.

Linney tore the game console out of the wall and threw it across the room. She called me a lot of bad names.

I'd write them down in here, but I can't spell them. They were really bad though.

Mommy always called me "little Benny."

Daddy always called me "champ" and said that I was a good boy.

There was a knock on my door.

"Yes?" I asked.

"Open the door," Linney said.

The tone of her voice told me that I needed to open the door quickly.

"Yes, Mommy?" I asked.

She had some swelling around her eyes. Lips. Her eyes looked black.

Linney backhanded me.

"That was for getting me hit, too. Now, get your ass to bed before I beat you, too."

I went to my bed and closed my eyes.

I knew that if I cried; at least, where she could hear me she would hit me worse.

She'd done it before.

Chapter Ten

September 16, 2016

Linney left me with the neighbor girl, Angela, again. She has been gone for a few days now. We're by ourselves.

Angela told me to stay in my room and only called me out when it was time to eat.

She did have me brush my teeth and made sure that I took my baths. Made sure that I did my homework.

Most of the time, I was by myself. Angela always had friends over until late.

Sometimes it was hard to sleep.

I wrote in my journal a lot.

Today's entry read:

Linney is gone. She has been gone for a couple of days right now. Angela is staying with me.

She doesn't pay attention to me. She always has friends over. Usually it's a bunch of boys.

Angela does make sure that I eat, do my homework, brush my teeth, and take a bath.

Even though she doesn't like to, she stays in the bathroom with me while I take one.

I think it's because she notices the bruises. I think she wants to ask me questions, but is afraid to at the same time. I think if she knew that Linney beat me then she would say something.

I would be too afraid to tell her or anyone else the truth anyway.

At least once a week, Linney would threaten to kill me.

I believed her.

Linney still scares me.

"Brendan!" Angela called. "Breakfast!"

I closed my journal, put it in it's hiding place, and went into the kitchen.

"French toast," she said, as I sat down.

"Thank you," I said, taking a couple of slices.

"You're welcome. Brendan?"

"Yeah?"

"I know that I don't watch you like I should, but I do care about you. You can still tell me anything, okay?"

I didn't look at her. "Okay. I know."

"Okay then. Hurry up. Your bus should be here soon."

"Did you hear from my mom?"

"Not yet, buddy."

I nodded and looked out the window. I ate quickly.

Chapter Eleven

When I got home from school that day, Angela wasn't in the living room. She was always waiting in the living room with door slightly open, just in case she had to go the bathroom or was in the kitchen. That way I knew she was there.

"Angela?" I called. "Mommy?"

I didn't get an answer. I went to my room and put my backpack down in there. Mommy didn't like anything in the living room that didn't belong there. I noticed that my mom's door was open, but I knew better than to go in there when she wasn't home.

Maybe Angela had gone home for a minute.

She lived right next door.

I knocked on the front door and it opened on it's own.

"Mrs. Rollins? Angela?" I called. "Hello?"

I went into each room and I finally found Mrs. Rollins in her bedroom. She was naked and tied to her bed. She was looking right at me, but she wasn't saying anything.

I went back into the kitchen and picked up the phone. I called 911.

Chapter Twelve

"911, what's your emergency?" the operator asked.

"Hi," I said.

"What's your name?"

"Brendan."

"Do you know your address?"

"No. I'm at my neighbor's house. My babysitter wasn't there, so I came over to her home. Her mommy is tied up to her bed. She doesn't have clothes on. I still can't find Angela."

"How old are you, Brendan?"

"Five years old."

"Can you stay on the phone with me?"

"Okay. Mrs. Rollins has her eyes open, but she didn't say anything when I came into her room."

"Okay, Brendan. You're doing good. Where's your mom at?"

I started to cry. "I don't know. She left me home with Angela."

"It's okay. The officers are on their way, you should be able to hear the sirens soon. Just stay on the phone with me."

"Okay." I heard the sirens.

"They're there?"

I sniffled. "Yes."

"Good. Hang up and go outside to let them know where you are."

"Okay."

I hung up the phone and ran outside. I was waving my arms around in the air.

* * *

There were two police cars and an ambulance and a fire truck. If I wasn't so scared it would have been cool.

Four policemen and two fireman came towards me.

"Are you Brendan?" one of the officers asked.

"Yes," I replied.

"I'm Officer Platt and this is my partner Officer Devine. The two officers behind us are Officers Park and Blaine. The fireman are Fireman Lynch and Fireman Cragan."

I waved.

"They're going to check your house. Which one is it?" I pointed. "Your neighbor's house?"

"Behind me."

"Good. Why don't you come and sit with me in my car. Tell me what happened."

"Okay."

The officer, Platt, held out his hand and I took it. He led me to his car and opened the back door for me.

"Okay, Brendan. What happened?"

"I got home from school and my front door was open all the way. I went in. Angela usually leaves it open so I know that she's in there, but its not usually open that much. That far, I mean. I went straight to my room and I put my backpack down. I called for Angela and when she didn't call back, I called for Mommy. I still didn't get an answer."

"What then?"

"I noticed that my Mommy's room was open, I didn't go in. I'm not allowed. I left. When I got to Angela's house, I knocked on the door. It opened. I called out to her or her mom. When they didn't call back, I went to each room."

"All right."

"I found Mrs. Rollins in her bedroom. Her eyes were open. She didn't have clothes on. She was tied up. Mrs. Rollins didn't say anything. I still can't find Angela."

"Did you touch anything?"

I nodded. "I went into the kitchen after I found Mrs. Rollins. I used the phone."

"Where's your mom?"

I shrugged. "I don't know."

"Can anyone stay with you until we find her?"

I started crying. "I don't know."

"Shh. Shh. It's okay. Does Angela have a dad?"

"Yes. He's usually at work all day. Her brother, too. He works after school."

"Good. Why don't you hang out here?"

"Okay."

The officer left and was gone a long time.

Chapter Thirteen

"Brendan?" Officer Platt said. "We're going to take you to your house to grab a few things, okay?"

"Did you find Angela?" I asked. I was really worried. "Or my mom?"

"We did. Angela's dad is coming to pick you up. We're going to meet him at the police station."

"Okay." Something was wrong.

They took me into the house. They'd been in my mom's room. I'd get smacked for that.

I went to my room. I grabbed some clothes, a coat, my journal, and backpack.

Officer Platt put me in his car and we drove off.

* * *

Mr. Rollins arrived later. He'd been crying. Angela's brother, Eric was with him. He'd been crying, too.

I was sitting in a room with a glass window that faced into the hall and a round table with chairs in the middle of the room. That's how I could see Mr. Rollins and Eric.

The door had been left open a little bit so that I could call for Officer Platt if I needed something.

On the way here he'd bought me a hamburger and fries with a soda.

"What do you mean I have to take him?" Mr. Rollins asked. *"My wife and daughter are dead! Raped!"*

What did he mean, Mrs. Rollins and Angela were gone? Did he mean dead? I thought. *No! No! No!*

I knew what dead meant. I didn't know what gone meant.

"Did he see anyone strange in the neighborhood today?

"No, sir."

"Did you ask him?"

"Yes, on our way here. If you don't take him he'll be placed with a foster family."

"Do that. I don't want to take him."

Officer Platt sighed.

Mr. Rollins and Eric left; Officer Platt took out his phone.

Chapter Fourteen

September 25, 2016

Mr. Rollins never came back for me.

When Officer Platt had made that phone call, it was to his wife. She, Jane, agreed to take me in while they tried to locate Linney.

"Good morning, Brendan," Jane said, knocking on the door. "Wake up."

"Good morning, Jane," I replied. She had insisted to being called by her first name. She felt old otherwise. "Did you sleep okay?"

"Good. What about you?"

"Very well."

She nodded and smiled. "Get dressed and grab your backpack. I'm gonna take you to school."

"Okay."

I'd been with the Platts for almost a week now, maybe longer, and they still hadn't found my mother.

"Do you think they'll find my mother?"

"Yes. Soon."

I smiled. "Okay."

I sat down at the table. There was toast and eggs. Hash browns and sausage for breakfast. Orange juice and milk as well.

Jane made me a plate and sat it in front of me. Then she poured me a glass of milk when there was a very loud knock on the front door.

"Here you go, sweetie." Jane sat the milk in front of me and went to answer the door. "Hello?"

"Where the fuck is my son?" Linney demanded. "You stole him!"

"Miss, you need to call the police station. You can't just come and take him. You left him."

"With a babysitter! He wasn't alone! Brendan!"

I grabbed my backpack and ran to the front door. "Mommy!" I exclaimed.

I started towards Linney, but Jane grabbed my arm. I was in between them. "You can't take him."

Linney grabbed my other arm and held it tightly. It would bruise. "Ow, you're hurting me."

Jane let go and Linney just glared at me. "Car. Now. We're going home."

I nodded and left.

I didn't look towards Jane. I'd cry and Linney would only smack me and beat me harder.

Chapter Fifteen

We didn't return to the house. As a matter-of-fact, we drove right out of Kona.

Linney didn't stop for gas or food. We didn't have any clothes with us. Nothing.

"Mom?" I asked.

"Don't you say a fucking word, Brendan," she replied. I knew by the tone of her voice that she meant it. I didn't say another word.

After an hour, she finally pulled over. It was in a slightly wooded area.

"What did you tell them?" she demanded, shutting the car off.

"Nothing, Mom."

"Why did they take you?"

"Someone had broken into our house and killed Angela. Raped her. Then they went next door and killed Mrs. Rollins. They tied her up. Raped her, too. What's rape?"

She backhanded me. Hard. "Fucking liar!"

I shook my head. "I promise. I never said anything about you except that I didn't know where you were! I told the truth. Only Angela knew!"

Linney grabbed my leg and pinched me hard.

"Mommy! Stop!"

She smacked me down there.

"Come on you little punk, cry! Cry like the little punk ass bitch you are! I dare you. Cry!"

Linney smacked me down there again.

I didn't cry.

She undid my belt, pulled me over to her, and laid me over her knees. She pulled my pants down, baring my bottom. She smacked it as hard as she could.

Chapter Sixteen

Linney put me back in my seat, buckled me up. We finally went home.

When we returned the house, Officer Platt and Jane were there. Jane looked upset and nervous.

"Don't say a fucking word," Linney said, through her teeth. "We went for a drive. If you show any pain then next time I'll come back from the woods alone."

"Okay, Mommy," I said.

We pulled into the driveway.

Officer Platt came to the passenger side of the car and opened the door.

"Hi, Brendan," he said.

"Hi, Officer Platt," I replied, cheerily. "Did you bring my clothes?"

"No, buddy."

"Why not?"

"What are you doing here there?" Linney asked, getting out of the car.

"Ms. Sanders, we need to take Brendan with us."

"Why?"

"A judge needs to sign off on you getting Brendan back."

"Why?"

"Your babysitter was killed in your home, in your bed. Raped. Her mother suffered the same fate. Brendan was left with no one. You were gone with no way to contact you. You were gone for almost a week."

"Well..."

Officer Platt shook his head. "No. Nothing. Brenda, get your backpack."

"I want to stay with Mommy."

Jane stepped forward. "I know you do. Let's get

your bag, sweetie. You can be with Mommy in a couple of days."

I went to the car and got my backpack. Linney tried to grab for me, but Officer Platt stopped her. "No. I don't want to have to arrest you."

"I'll see you in a few days, baby."

"Okay, Mommy."

"Remember what I said?"

"Yes, Mommy. I love you, too."

"Good boy."

Jane took my hand and led me to their car.

I was finally free of Linney, but for how long.

Chapter Seventeen

I opened my journal and read:

Linney beat me today.

She smacked me twice in my private area.

I want to tell someone, but she said she would kill me.

I believed her.

I'm back with Officer Platt and Jane while Linney goes to court to get me back. Not that being with them is a good thing. It shows me what love and caring is. Reminds me of my Mommy and Daddy. I miss them!

Another entry read:

Back with Linney. We're home. She beat me again.

A wooden spoon on my bare bottom.

It hurt so bad!

I don't know why she keeps beating me. Hitting me. I don't do anything wrong!

I've had a lot of chances to say who I really am. Was. Whatever. I never do. I never say anything.

I even made sure that Jane never saw what Linney had done to my private area. How bad she hit me there. It still hurts. It's all red and swollen.

It was very difficult to do.

* * *

Linney entered the bathroom while I was taking a bath.

"Almost done?" she asked, closing the lid on the toilet and sitting down. "What is that? What happened?"

"What?" I asked, confused.

"With your private area."

"You don't like when I tell you the truth. When I remind you of the pain you did."

"Honey, what happened?"

"It's from when you hit me in the car."

"Oh, honey."

She stood up, grabbed a towel, pulled me out of the tub. She quickly toweled me off and put me in pajamas.

"When we get there, I want you to say you were attacked."

"Okay."

We got into the car and went to the hospital.

Chapter Eighteen

The doctor called the police and Linney was arrested.

I didn't say anything. It was the perfect chance.

"Did she hurt you, Brendan?" Jane asked.

Officer Platt was at work.

"No, Jane," I replied. "I was attacked. I didn't see who did it. Neither did my mommy."

"Sweetie, I know that's what you said, but it had to have happened when you left here. You should have beat us to your house. It's not far. You were gone for over an hour."

"Mommy took me to get food and then we went to the park."

"Honey, I don't think that's the truth."

I looked at her, tears welling up in my eyes. I was scared. I wanted to be a good boy. I wanted to tell the truth. I couldn't. "Jane, even if it wasn't I would never say anything."

"If she's hurting you…"

I shook my head. "Please, don't make me."

I started crying.

"Oh, Brendan."

"Just let me go. Let me go home."

"I…"

"Please, Jane. I want my mommy."

I clung to her as I cried.

Chapter Nineteen

The journal entry that I'd just written, read:

Mommy and Daddy must have been really so scared and sad when I died.

I wish I could tell them that I was alive. That I was okay.

Well, not okay. I didn't want to lie to them. I was alive. I was a good boy. It didn't matter what Linney said.

It didn't matter what Linney did to me.

I was a good boy.

Jane respected my wishes. She stopped asking me if Linney had hurt me or been hurting me. She even got Officer Platt to stop asking me, too.

He said that I could go home in a day or two. He wasn't happy about it, but he didn't have a choice.

Chapter Twenty

October 1, 2016

Linney and I went on vacation. We took a plane.

We were gone for two whole weeks!

She'd surprised me when we got home.

We'd gone to Disneyland!

I had pictures with Goofy and Donald Duck. Mickey and Minnie Mouse.

I got to ride Dumbo and Mr. Toads Wild Ride. Pirates of the Caribbean. The Haunted Mansion. It's a Small World After All.

Linney hated that ride! The song really bugged her.

We rode the tea cups. I didn't get sick, but Linney did! It took everything I had not laugh.

We ate frozen lemonade and got Mickey ears. We drank soda and enjoyed the parades.

We went to San Diego.

I saw Shamu. Road a water ride. Saw sea lions and fish.

We went to Knott's Berry Farm.

We played in the arcade. Ate a bunch.

Linney even took me to Universal Studios.

We rode the trams and saw things from movies.

It was awesome.

* * *

We returned home. It was late, so Linney and I went straight to bed. We didn't even unpack the car.

I woke up early.

I decided to write in my journal since I hadn't been able to in two weeks. I didn't want Linney to know that I had it.

It was going to be a good entry, maybe entries. Not bad ones.

It read:

Ben Delta   Marie Garcia

We went to Disneyland!

Linney felt so bad about what happened that she booked us for two weeks.

I asked if we'd got bored of Disneyland what could we do.

She laughed and said, "Who gets bored of Disneyland?"

"Well?"

"There's Knott's Berry Farm. Universal Studios. Sea Worled and California Adventure."

"Okay."

We arrived late the first day, so the park was already closed, but we were the first ones in line the next morning.

First, we went on a couple of rides. We bought Mickey ears and some candy.

We rode the Pirates of the Caribbean and Haunted Mansion. Dumbo. Mr. Toad's Wild Ride. Dumbo, again. It's a Small World.

Linney let me take pictures with Mickey and Minnie. Goofy. Donald Duck.

I had so much fun!

I did miss my mommy and daddy and wished that I could have been there with them though. Milo and Elliott would have had so much fun!

The next entry read:

Today, we drove down to San Diego.

We went to Sea World and the zoo!

First, we went to Sea World, though.

I saw Shamu and he splashed us so much.

There were sea lions and fish.

A walrus.

We only stayed for a short time. Half the day.

I missed the frozen lemonade at Disneyland. It was so good!

We stopped for a quick hamburger. Linney let me eat in the car. I was really careful about not making a mess.

The zoo was fun, too.

The lions were my favorite.

The penguins, too. I loved the way the waddled. So cute.

The polar bears liked to dance in the water. They were so big.

  We got back to Anahiem fairly late. So, we went right to bed. There was still a lot of Disneyland to see and California Adventure. Plus Knott's Berry Farm.

  The next entry read:

  Today was Knott's Berry Farm.

  There was an arcade and a bakery.

  A few rides.

  It wasn't as much fun as Sea World or Disneyland. Or even the zoo!

  The food was nice though.

  The arcade was neat.

  The next entry read:

  We went to Universal Studios today and it was okay.

  There was a diner that looked like it was from the 50s! At least, that's what Linney said. I wasn't sure.

  We took a tram tour and a shark jumped out! That was scary, but a good scary.

  Everyone laughed about it afterwards.

  I'm glad that Linney took me. It was a lot of fun.

It made me forget about what she did and what happened to Angela and Mrs. Rollins.

Chapter Twenty-One

"Good morning," Linney called.

I put my journal away and went into the living room.

"Good morning," I said, cheerfully.

"We'll have breakfast and then I'll take you to school."

"Okay, Mommy. Do we have any cereal?"

"Let's look." We headed into the kitchen. She went to the cupboards, and I went to the fridge.

"I'll get the milk."

"Okay." She began opening the cupboards.

"No milk."

"No cereal. Go get dressed and we'll head to McDonald's for a quick one. Then head to school. Okay?"

"Okay, Mommy."

I ran down the hall to my room and quickly looked through my drawers for clean clothes. I put on a blue striped shirt with a collar and a pair of dark blue jeans.

Linney got me an egg sandwich with cheese and hash browns. I don't know why it was called 'hash browns' there was only a shredded potato patty. Not a lot of them.

I also had orange juice.

Chapter Twenty-Two

Janey came up to me after I got to my classroom.

"Hi," she said.

"Hi, Janey," I replied. "Another dare?"

"No. You missed a lot of school. Are you okay?"

"Yes. Why?"

"Just making sure. Bye."

That was really weird.

* * *

"Brendan," my teacher said, smiling. "Welcome back. How are you?"

"Good," I replied, happily.

"How was your vacation?"

"So much fun. I hope we can go to Disney World next time!"

"That would be fun. We can talk during recess."

"Sure." I smiled and went to my desk.

We learned a lot about science. Animals. Lions and bears. The food pyramid.

In PE we did a lot of running and jump rope. I liked jump rope.

Chapter Twenty-Three

"Brendan?" my teacher asked, as we came back from recess.

"Yes," I replied.

"The principal wants to see you."

"Okay."

I took the pass that she handed to me and I left the classroom and went to the office. "Hi!" I said, smiling brightly.

I liked the office. The secretary was so nice and always smiling. Even if there was a student in trouble.

"Hi, Brendan," the secretary said, smiling. She knew everyone's names. We all liked her so much.

You didn't mind getting sent here, even if you were in trouble. "What can I do for you?"

I handed her my paper. "My teacher said that the principal wanted to see me."

She took the paper. "Go right in."

"Thank you!"

She waved at me as I walked past the desk and to the principal's office.

* * *

I knocked on the door. You always knock on a door before entering. Even if the person on the other side knows that you're coming. It's just being polite.

"Come in," he called. He was looking up as I entered his office. "Ah, Brendan! Come in. Here have a seat."

"My teacher said that you wanted to talk to me."

"Yes. I understand that you've missed a lot of school lately."

"Yes, sir."

"Why?"

"My neighbor and babysitter were killed. Mommy wanted to distract me. We went to Disneyland."

"What did you do there?"

"I got pictures with Mickey and Minnie Mouse. Ate frozen a lot of frozen lemonade. It was so yummy. Rode Dumbo. Haunted Mansion."

"That sounds fun. What else?"

"We went to Sea World and saw Shamu. That's a whale. Killer whale. Orca. He splashed us!"

"How funny."

"It was."

"What else?"

"We went to Universal Studios. A shark scared us. We all laughed."

"Brendan, would you mind talking to Miss Ellis?"

"The counselor? Why?"

"Well, so she can make sure you're okay. You can talk about your neighbor and your babysitter."

"I guess so. Does Mommy know?"

"Yes."

"Okay."

He picked up his phone and spoke into it.
"She'll be right here."

I nodded and waited.

Chapter Twenty-Four

"Hi, Miss Ellis," I said.

"Hello, Brendan," she replied. "Come with me."

"Okay. Bye."

"Bye, Brendan," the principal said.

Miss Ellis held out her hand and I took it.

We went to her office.

She had a table in the middle of the room. She had bookcases that were filled with games and puzzles.

She had some dolls.

Legos.

"So, the principal is a little concerned about you," Miss Ellis said.

"How come?" I asked.

"Well, you found your neighbor…"

"Mrs. Rollins."

"Yes, dead."

"Yes. Her eyes were open."

"How did that make you feel?"

"It was weird."

"Why?"

"Well, Mrs. Rollins was naked. She was looking right at me and she didn't ask me to leave. She was tied up, too. She didn't ask me to help her."

"Oh, Brendan."

"I never saw Angela again."

"Did you realize Mrs. Rollins was dead?"

"Not until I heard Officer Platt and Mr. Rollins talking about it at the police station."

"How did you hear that?"

"Officer Platt had left the door to the room open. In case I needed him."

"Did you need him?"

"No. He bought me a hamburger and a soda."

"That was nice."

"Yep."

"Are you okay? Your mom was gone a long time."

"Yeah. She's done it before. That's why I had Angela."

"Did you like Angela?"

"Sure."

"Why?"

I looked at her, thoughtfully.

Chapter Twenty-Five

"Brendan, why did you like Angela?" Miss Ellis asked.

"Well, she let me stay in my room," I said. "She would cook me dinner. Let me go outside."

"She watch you?"

"Yes. No."

"Why yes?"

"She was there."

"Why no?"

"Angela always had boys over. Usually more when she was watching me for more than one day."

"Why?"

I shrugged. "Maybe her Mom didn't like them playing in the bed."

"Playing?"

"They took their clothes off. Angela would play with his private part. He played with hers. Well, they would. Some times she would be with more than one boy at a time. Some times she would be with two or more boys at one time."

"Brendan, how do you know that?"

"I'm not supposed to be in Mommy's room when she's not there, but I like to hide in her closet some times. It's some times quiet in there."

"So, you would watch them...play?"

"Some times. Most of the time, I would just lie down and cover my ears. Go to sleep."

"Why?"

"They would scream a lot."

"Oh."

"Officer Platt, no, Mr. Rollins said that Angela and Mrs. Rollins were raped. What does that mean? Mommy won't, well, wouldn't tell me."

"Unless your Mommy says it's okay, I can't tell you."

"Okay."

"Well, thank you for talking to me. You can go back to class."

"Thank you."

I got up and left the room.

Chapter Twenty-Six

Linney picked me up after school.

"Hi, Mommy!" I exclaimed, getting into the car. "How was your day?"

"Good," Linney replied, smiling. "You have a good day?"

"Yep."

"We need to go grocery shopping before we go home."

"Okay. Can we Lucky Charms or Trix?"

"Sure. You can get both."

"Yay!"

"Did the principal talk to you?"

"Yes. Good you did know."

"Yes." She looked at me. "Did you think that I didn't?"

"I wasn't sure. I wasn't going to talk to him if you didn't know."

"Okay. What did you talk about?"

"He asked why I was gone. I told him that we went to Disneyland. Sea World."

"Did the counselor talk to you?"

"Yes."

"What about?"

"Mrs. Rollins. Angela. She wanted to make sure I was okay, I guess."

"Oh. Okay. What should we do for dinner?"

"Homemade pizza or spaghetti."

"How about we do spaghetti tonight and then pizza tomorrow?"

"Yay!"

Linney laughed as we pulled away from the school and headed to the grocery store.

Chapter Twenty-Seven

"Brendan, can you go grab the cereal you want?" Linney asked, grabbing a cart. "You can get three boxes. You said you wanted Trix and Lucky Charms, right?"

"Yes, Mommy. Can I get Apple Jacks?"

"Of course. Do you remember where the produce is?"

"Yes, Mommy." I turned and pointed. "That way. At the end."

"Right. Meet me there."

"Okay. I'll race you."

Linney laughed. "Just be careful."

I grinned up at her and ran to get the cereal.

* * *

I couldn't reach the Apple Jacks, so the clerk in the aisle helped me.

"Thank you," I said, running off.

I found Linney in produce. "Hi, Mommy," I said. "Got it."

"Good boy," Linney said. "Can you grab two cans of diced and crushed tomatoes? One can of sliced black olives?"

"Sure. Will you be here?"

"Yes. If not, I'll be two aisles that way."

She pointed.

"Okay."

I walked to the aisle with the tomatoes and found the crushed tomatoes first. I grabbed two cans. Then I found the diced tomatoes, two shelves over, and grabbed two cans. Then I went to the next aisle and grabbed one can of the sliced black olives.

I went to the aisle Linney was. She took the cans and put them in the cart.

"Can you grab one pizza crust and one box of spaghetti?"

"Yes."

"I'll be in the aisle next to this."

"Okay."

I went and grabbed the noodles and pizza crust.

I found Linney and she put the items in the cart.

"Almost done. We just need milk and eggs."

"Okay."

We headed towards where the milk was.

"Would you like dessert?"

"Could we get the three flavor ice cream and chocolate syrup?"

"Sure. Can you grab it and meet me at the milk?"

"Okay."

I grabbed the chocolate syrup first and then the ice cream. I really only liked the chocolate and strawberry, but they did taste good together.

Linney was standing next to the milk and she was talking to someone.

She looked upset.

Chapter Twenty-Eight

Linney was shaking her head at the person and they left.

I moved towards her. The man, I didn't like him.

"Here, Mommy," I said.

"All set?" she asked.

"Yes, ma'am."

"Good."

We headed to the check out line and loaded up the belt.

I knew better than to ask her questions.

We paid for our things, loaded the cart back up, and left.

As we exited the building, Linney kept looking around. We quickly loaded the car with our food and toilet paper. Laundry detergent and left.

* * *

We got home and took the groceries inside the house. Linney locked the door once we were inside.

"Go get started on your homework, buddy," she said, loading the groceries onto the counter. "I'll put this away and start dinner."

"Okay, Mommy," I said.

I grabbed my backpack and went into my room.

I could hear her in the kitchen, speaking softly to herself, as she put things away.

Because we were gone for two weeks, I did have a lot of homework.

I saw that my suitcase was sitting on my bed. I put my backpack on my desk. I pulled the suitcase off the bed and started emptying it.

I put the dirty clothes in the hamper, and my souvenirs all around the room. Then I started my homework.

I couldn't believe how much there was to do.

Chapter Twenty-Nine

I opened my journal for a quick entry.

It read:

Linney and I just got back from the grocery store.

Something weird happened. She doesn't know that I saw, but there was someone there. Someone she ran into.

I don't know if she knew him from home or what.

She was upset.

I didn't ask questions.

I never do.

At least, not about her personal or adult problems.

Time for homework before dinner.

* * *

"Brendan!" Linney called. "Dinner. Go wash up."

"Okay," I replied, putting my homework away. "Heading to the bathroom. Be right out."

"Good boy."

I washed and dried my hands. I made sure to wipe out the sink and hang the towel back up.

"Did you need me to set the table?"

"Sure. Let me get the plates."

"Okay. I'll grab the napkins and silverware. The place mats, too."

"Thanks."

I went to the drawer. I grabbed two forks, two spoons, and two butter knives. I grabbed two napkins and two place mats. "Mommy, we need glasses, too."

"Oh, right."

I sat the items on the table and went to grab the plates.

"Thank you. Remember the knives go on the left."

"Okay, Mommy."

I put the place mats down, one in front of each chair. I put the plates in the center with the knives to the left of the plates and the spoons and the forks on the right. The napkin was folded in half, neatly and placed underneath the fork and spoon.

Linney handed me the glasses and I sat them down.

"Take a seat. I'll bring the food to the table."

"Okay, Mommy."

I sat in my seat. I waited patiently for her to plate the food.

It smelled so good.

Chapter Thirty

October 3, 2016

A couple days had passed since we'd returned from Disneyland. I woke up early again.

I opened my journal to a blank page and began to write.

It read:

Linney hit me again. Pretty bad.

I was clearing the dishes. The dinner plate that I'd picked up fell out of my hand.

It broke.

Linney grabbed me by the neck and threw me against the wall

She immediately felt horrible about it.

I didn't cry.

I knew better. Crying only made things worse.

* * *

After I finished my entry, I got started on my homework. There was so much to do. I wanted to try to get as much done as I could before school this morning.

Hopefully, I could get through it all.

"Brendan?" Linney asked, knocking on the door. "Are you up?"

"It's unlocked," I said, closing my book. "Yes, I'm up."

Linney opened the door. "Are you okay?"

"Yes. I was just trying to get caught up on my homework."

"Okay. Breakfast in ten minutes."

"Okay."

She closed the door and I got ready for school.

Chapter Thirty-One

Olivia and Noah ran up to me at recess.

"Are you okay?" Noah asked. He and Olivia were twins. "You're walking weird."

"Yeah," Olivia added. "You're limping."

Noah was an inch taller and a minute older. You wouldn't know it though. He let Olivia boss him around all the time.

I wish my sisters were around to boss me around.

I'm sure that if they were here and were actually bossing me around that I wouldn't like it, but at least they'd be around.

"I'm okay," I said, lying. "I slept funny. My leg was hanging over the edge of the bed. My mom said it would get better as the day goes on. Probably be all better by tomorrow."

"How was Disneyland?"

"Fun. I'm going to bring in my Mickey ears for show and tell."

"Cool."

The teacher called us in from recess for lunch.

* * *

When I got home, Linney wasn't there.

I put my backpack in my bedroom and went next door. Like I was supposed to do.

I knocked on the door. This time the door didn't open on it's own.

"Yes?" a man asked.

"It's Brendan," I replied. "My mom wasn't home. I'm supposed to come over here when she's not there. Especially when there babysitter isn't there."

"She went to pick something up." The door opened. "Come on in. Don't touch anything."

Eric opened the door an I went into the living room and sat down on the couch; waiting for Linney to return.

Chapter Thirty-Two

There was a knock on the door a couple of hours later.

Eric got up and answered it.

"Hello, Eric," Linney said.

"Hello, Linney," he replied. I was the only person not allowed to call her by her name. I had to call her mom.

"Is Brendan here?"

"The living room."

"Come on Brendan!"

"Coming," I called.

I got up and went to the door.

"Thank you for keeping an eye on him." She opened her purse and pulled out some money. "Here. How are you and your father doing?"

"We're okay. Thank you for asking."

"We're having homemade pizza tonight. You're more than welcome to come and join us."

"Thank you. I'll ask Dad when he gets home."

"Great. See you later."

I waved to Eric and we went home.

* * *

An hour later, there was a knock on the door.

"Yes?" I called.

I'd been working on my homework since we got home.

I was almost done.

"Eric and Mr. Rollins are here," Linney said, opening the door. "Come out."

"Okay, Mommy."

I closed my book and followed her out to the living room.

Chapter Thirty-Three

"Welcome," I said, entering the living room. "How are you, Mr. Rollins?"

"Doing okay," he replied. "Thank you for asking. How are you doing? I'm sorry that I didn't bring you back with me."

"It's okay."

"Can I help set the table?" Eric asked.

"Sure," Linney said. "Plates are there. Cups and silverware. Place mats. Napkins."

"Okay."

I excused myself to go wash my hands. Dinner was almost ready.

* * *

Linney made a great pizza. There wasn't any left!

Eric cleared the table and Mr. Rollins did the dishes.

I excused myself to go do my homework.

A little while later, there was a knock on my door.

"Yes?" I asked.

"It's Mom," Linney said.

"It's open."

Linney came in and sat on my bed. "What was that about?"

"What, Mommy?"

"What Mr. Rollins said?"

"Oh. He didn't want to bring me home. That's why I had to stay with Officer Platt."

"Why didn't he want to take you?"

"I don't know, Mommy. I didn't get a chance to talk to him. Officer Platt did. Do you think that Mr. Rollins was mad at me?"

"No. Of course not. Why would you think that?"

I looked at her. Very seriously. "Because he didn't take me from the police station when he left."

"Oh, sweetie, he was probably just upset. Angela and Mrs. Rollins had just died."

"Okay."

"How's your homework coming?"

"Almost done."

"Really? Two weeks worth?"

"Yes, ma'am. I've been waking up early since we got back. Must still be on vacation time. I put it to good use."

"Well, good for you. I'm so proud of you!"

"Thank you, Mommy."

"I'm going to go take a shower and then go to bed. I want you in bed before I get out."

"Yes, Mommy."

Chapter Thirty-Four

October 10, 2016

I woke up early again. I pulled out my journal. I flipped the pages until I found the earlier entry that I wanted.

It read:

I'm really missing my brothers and sisters today. All of my kids in my class were able to eat lunch with their brother or sister. I felt left out.

For some reason, I felt guilt and shame.

There was no reason for that.

Some times, I can still see Willow and Amethyst and Milo and Elliott as they struggled for their last breaths. I can still hear them coughing.

I missed them so much.

I hoped that Tess and Aria and Sage and Emerald were okay.

Wait, the news had said that Aria was gone, too. Dead.

I don't remember her being there. I clearly remember someone picking her up before the fire started.

I hope they were okay.

I love them so much.

* * *

I put my journal away and decided to lay back down.

I wasn't feeling well. My stomach hurt on the right side.

"Brendan?" Linney asked, knocking. "Honey?"

"Mommy?" I replied. "My tummy hurts."

"What happened?"

Linney came and sat down next to me on the bed. She felt my head.

"I don't know. I was up early again. I did some reading. When I was done. I felt funny, so I laid back down."

"You're burning up." She got up. "Let me get dressed. We'll go to urgent care."

"Okay."

Linney quickly got dressed and came back for me. She picked me up. She had her purse and keys. She just ran out the door with me.

Chapter Thirty-Five

"Did you have an appointment?" the nurse asked.

Why would we need an appointment? It's the emergency room? I thought. I'd been to one before.

"No," Linney replied. "I went to go get him up for breakfast. He said that his tummy hurt. I felt his forehead. He's burning up. We went to urgent care first and they sent us here."

"Okay. Name?"

"Brendan Sanders."

"Bring him back."

We had went to the doctor's office first, like Linney had said. They checked my temperature which was 101.6 and they told us to come straight to the emergency room.

Linney answered the same questions a couple of more times with the different nurses that came into the room before the doctor came in.

"What's wrong?" she asked.

"Good thing you brought him in," the doctor said.

He seemed nicer than the last time I was here.

"Why?"

"It looks like an appendicitis. We're going to take him to surgery."

"Oh, God."

"Don't worry. Any longer and it would have, could have, been a lot worse."

"Oh…"

"Don't worry. He's safe and in good hands. Any allergies?"

"No. Not that I know of."

'Okay. I'll come and get you when he's in recovery. I know it's hard, but try to relax. He'll be okay."

"Thanks."

* * *

The surgery went well.

I was moved to a private room. Linney wasn't able to stay with me this time either. Rules.

Mr. Rollins and Eric came to visit me while I was in the hospital.

Even Mrs. Rollins and Angela never did that.

I really like them. Mr. Rollins and Eric.

Chapter Thirty-Six

January 11, 2017

After my surgery and recovery, Linney began acting strange. Even for her.

She told me that her head was hurting a lot and she was gone a lot more than she was before.

Eric and Mr. Rollins let me stay with them after school and some times I would stay overnight. Whenever Linney was going to be late.

I was getting worried.

I mean, I didn't like her a lot of the time. You know, she kidnapped me, but I did care about her. She was taking care of me. When she wasn't hitting me or throwing me across the room.

She seemed to be having a hard time eating and drinking. She couldn't keep anything down. She was losing weight.

Linney wasn't a very big woman to begin with.

* * *

I was home tonight. Eric was staying with me at my house tonight.

He watched me better than Angela did. He also didn't have friends over.

I decided to write in my journal.

It read:

Eric has become a favorite babysitter! He helped me with my homework. Angela didn't. He cooked so good.

Better than Linney.

Don't tell her.

When I'd go outside, he would go with me. We played catch. Sometimes we'd play basketball or soccer.

It was weird staying at his house. I had never stayed overnight at someone's house before. I'd only stayed at Disneyland or the hotel on the way here.

Eric's house was creepy at night. There were weird noises. Figures.

Anyway, Linney said we were going to be moving.

I don't know when. I don't know why. I don't even know where.

All Linney will tell me is that it's a good thing and not to worry. That it will all be okay.

I hope she was finally taking me home.

Linney had me stay with Eric and Mr. Rollins a lot now.

She kept taking things out of the house. Our memories.

The photos from Disneyland. My Mickey ears.

I,as always, kept my thoughts and questions to myself.

Linney never answered them anyway.

Chapter Thirty-Seven

February 3, 2017

Spokane, Washington

"Why are we here?" I asked.

I recognized the hotel we were at, vaguely.

I didn't understand what was going on. Linney had taken several days to pack up our home and put everything in a storage unit in Idaho. Before that she had packed us a small bag with just a few things in it. Enough for a couple of days.

"Mom?"

"I'm not your real mom, Brendon," she said. "Ben."

No duh! I thought.

"I rescued you, or so I thought from a house fire. This was three years ago. You were only three years old."

"Okay? My name is Brendan Hudson Sanders."

"I'm taking you back to your real parents. I am sick and I'm going to die. I don't want you to go to strangers."

"Mom?"

"No. Your name is Ben Delta. Your parents' names are Addyson and Haden Delta. You have sisters. Tessa and Sage and Emerald and Abbey and Melody. A couple of brothers."

Who were Abbey and Melody? My brothers died.

"I tried to find out all that I could. I tried to find their names, but I've forgotten. It's part of the disease."

"What's wrong?"

"I have an inoperable brain tumor and something else that I can't pronounce. I know that you think that I never cared about you. Never loved you. I don't blame you for thinking that. Believe me, I did."

"You hit me!"

"I know."

"A lot."

"I know."

"All of your boyfriends hit me, too."

"I know that, too."

"Also, a lot."

"I know."

"If you loved me, cared about, why did you do that? Why did you let them do that?"

"I don't know, Ben. I should have done this sooner. Once I realized that they had never meant for you to get hurt."

I looked out the window of the hotel.

"Can we get something to eat?"

"Sure. Order whatever you like. I'm not hungry."

I opened the phone book and called a local Italian place. I ordered a large pepperoni and sausage pizza with extra pepperoni and sausage; a spaghetti dinner. I also ordered cannoli and tiramisu.

* * *

My food arrived.

Linney had spent most of my wait time in the bathroom. I don't think she was feeling well.

I turned on the TV and a picture of my mother was on the news.

The report said:

"Decorated homicide detective, Addyson Delta was recently fired," the news anchor said. *"She was then re-hired after the apparent suicides of former partner, Jesus Meyers and her brother-in-law, Pagan Delta."*

"Uncle Pagan?" I whispered.

"Apparently, each man left a suicide note that will not be released to the public. Their families have asked for privacy and understanding during this time. The police department has not released a statement on the suicide of Detective Meyers and we're not likely to get one either. We do hope to speak with his father the warden of the Walla Walla prison."

"Tragic," her co-anchor said.

"Yes, it is."

"Any word as to why Detective Delta was fired?"

"No."

"Thank you. Now, the weather."

The door to the bathroom opened and Linney came back into the main room and sat down beside me.

Chapter Thirty-Eight

February 4, 2017
Vancouver, Washington

Linney and I had left the hotel and Spokane very early the next morning.

We didn't speak until we were about an hour away from Vancouver. I was finally home.

I was finally going to see my Mom and my Dad. My sisters.

Well, almost home.

"I am taking you to her job. You'll be safe there until she can come and get you," Linney said.

"Why won't you take me to the house?" I asked.

Because you're a coward? I thought. *Because you can get away from me faster at the police station?*

"I don't want to get caught." She took a piece of paper from her front pocket and handed it to me. "Give this to your mother. It explains everything."

I nodded. "Mom..."

She winced. "Call me Linney. I was a firefighter."

"Was that a tough job?"

"Yes. Not as hard of a job as your mother had. I can't imagine what she had to deal with."

"What do you mean?"

"Your mother is a very brave woman. Liked. Respected. Dealing with murderers has to be hard."

I looked out the window and thought about what she'd said. We didn't speak for the rest of the ride.

* * *

"We're here," Linney said.

I nodded and grabbed the bag between my legs that was on the floor. It contained my journal.

I got out of the car and closed the door. I was about to turn and tell her goodbye, when she drove off. She'd barely waited for me to close the door to leave. She couldn't wait to get out of here. She didn't even look in the rear view mirror.

I walked into the building.

"Can I help you?" the woman at the desk asked. "Where's your Mommy?"

"My name is Ben Delta," I said, proudly. I was glad to finally be able to say that out loud. "My mom is Addyson Delta. She works here. My dad is Haden Delta. My uncle is Terrence Delta. He works here, too."

The woman stared at me like she'd seen a ghost. Probably had. I'm sure that everyone thought I was dead. "Boss?" she said. "We have a situation out here. Bring Terrence, too."

A minute later, two men showed up at the desk. I recognized one of them immediately. He hadn't changed much.

"Uncle Terrence?"

"Who are you?" he asked, gently.

"It's me, Ben." I took the note out of my pocket. "This explains everything. I was supposed to give it to Mommy."

"Call Haden," the other man said. "What does the note say?"

"He's Ben. A firefighter found him and took him away. I'll call Haden."

"Let's go to my office, Ben. I'm Chief Mason Holmes. I'm your mom and uncle's boss. Your uncle is going to call your dad." He looked at Uncle Terrence. "Call Delia, too. Addyson will want a DNA test."

Terrence nodded and pulled out his phone.

Chapter Thirty-Nine

About half an hour later, the phone on Mason's desk rang.

"Send him back," he said. "Yes, her, too."

The door to his office opened and my daddy was suddenly there in front of me.

"Daddy!" I said, jumping up and launching myself into his arms. "I missed you! Where's Mommy?"

"Ben?" he asked, uncertain. "Why is Delia here?"

"I figured that Addyson would want a DNA test. This is so hard to believe," Mason answered. "We can get Delia to draw blood and put a rush on it."

"Okay." Dad removed me and had me take a seat. "This lady is going to take your blood, Ben. Then we'll talk about Mommy."

"Okay. I missed you."

There were tears in his eyes. "I missed you, too."

The nice lady smiled at me. She told me what she was going to do and then she did the same thing to Daddy. "It shouldn't take long. Addyson's blood is already in the system. If there's any match, it should come up right away."

"Thank you."

The woman left and Daddy turned to me. "What happened? Do you know?"

"Yes." I was finally able to tell everything. "I know I was a lot younger when you thought that I'd died."

Daddy nodded. "That's right. Amethyst, Willow, Milo, and Elliott died."

"Yes. Amethyst put me in a closet. They sat down and I heard them crying. After awhile, someone found me. A firefighter named Linney Sanders. She took me away. She said you two didn't deserve me. That you'd neglected me."

Daddy shook his head. "Your Mommy was in Boston with Delia and Sapphire. She needed a break after a bad couple of years at work."

I remembered what Linney had said about about it being difficult.

"She took me to Idaho. She beat me, some times. Her boyfriends beat me, some times, too."

"I'll kill her."

I shook my head. "She has a brain tumor. She's dying. I want my Mommy!"

"Mommy is in the hospital."

"Why? Does she have a brain tumor, too?"

"No. She's having a baby and it's been hard on her. She's going to be there until the baby is born."

"Is the baby okay?"

"Yes. You have some more siblings now. In addition to Tessa and Aria and Emerald and Sage you have sisters: Abby and Angela and Victoria and Aurora and Bayley and Amanda and Emilia Rose, and Sadie Mallory. You have some brothers too. They are

Jackson and Austin and Roman and Donovan Haden."

"Oh my!"

"Besides losing Elliott and Milo and Amethyst and Willow we lost some other babies. Jade and Braxton and Brittany and Oliver and Paizlie Jean."

"Oh, no!"

"Yeah. So, we're making sure we don't lose this baby, too."

"Okay. I want to see Mommy though."

"Of course."

"You're also an uncle."

"What?"

"Yeah. Tessa has two babies: Samantha and Miko. They're twins. Also Sage adopted three little ones: Brooke and Bobby and Brooklyn."

"Really?"

"Yep."

There was a knock on the door and the lady came in again.

"He's Ben."

Daddy looked at me and cried. He picked me up and we left.

Chapter Forty

"What is going on?" a girl asked. "Who is that?"

"Tessa," Daddy said. "You may want to sit down. You and Aria and Emerald and Sage won't believe it."

"Who is he?"

"It's Ben."

"NO!"

"Yes. Delia confirmed it."

"Benny?"

"Tessa! Oh, Tessa!" I exclaimed. I ran and jumped on my big sister, crying. "I missed you! It was horrible. I couldn't say who I was or anything. I was in the hospital once and wanted to say, but the Linney lady said she'd kill me!"

"Oh, Benny!"

Three other young ladies ran into the room upon hearing my name. "Benny?" one of them asked.

I looked at who'd spoken. "Aria?"

"Yes. How?"

"Amethyst put me in a closet to save me. She said that I needed to be protected. I heard them coughing and crying. It got so hot in the closet. There was white haze all through the house. Then it got quiet."

"Oh, God."

"Sage? Emerald?"

They waved. "We're so happy you're home!" they said, rushing towards me. They passed me around like I was a little doll.

This was love. This is what I missed.

"Can I meet my other siblings?"

"Sure."

"Everyone!"

When Daddy yelled, a bunch of little feet came running in.

Daddy introduced everyone in turn. I met everyone including Tessa and Sage's kids.

I was finally home, but there was one person missing.

I turned and looked at Daddy. "When can I see Mommy?"

"Tessa?"

"Sage and I got the kids. Take him to see Mom."

"Okay." He held his hand out to me. "We're going to go tomorrow. You need to rest and it's late. You and I are going to pick up dinner for everyone and then come back, watch a movie, hang out, and rest. Then first thing tomorrow we'll go. Okay?"

I yawned a little. "Okay."

Daddy laughed and we left.

Epilogue

February 5, 2017

My Dad, Haden Delta, knocked on the hospital door.

I heard a female voice yell, "Come in" through the door. When the door opened I heard the same voice say, "Oh, hey, honey. I wasn't expecting you. What's wrong?"

My dad walked into the room and looked behind him. I started to go with him and he put his hand up.

"Nothing," he replied. "It's good. Shocking, but good."

I heard a loud, constant beeping noise coming from the room as the door closed, but it stopped fairly quickly. "Please, just tell me."

Everything became muffled. I could still hear my Dad speaking to the person in the room. It was my Mom. She was pregnant and it was a rough pregnancy She was here to protect herself and the babies.

"Baby, he's alive," Dad said.

"Who?"

"Our baby. Our first baby."

"What? That's not possible. He—he died. Him and Milo. Elliott. The girls."

Dad must have moved further into the room, because his voice wasn't as clear as it was before. "I did a DNA test. They put a rush on it. He's our son. Your DNA was already on file."

"I want to see him."

"Yes?"

"Yes."

Dad opened the door and I started to walk in. I suddenly felt very shy. Awkward. So, I got a little defensive, maybe.

My mother, Addyson Delta, was sitting up in the hospital be. She was so beautiful.

"Ben?" she asked.

I nodded.

"How?"

"May I sit?" I asked.

"Yes."

Dad helped me onto the bed, even at six years old, it was still a little difficult to get up on the bed. He moved to the chair once I was on the bed. "According to the woman that I thought was my mother, the woman who has raised me these last years, she saw me hiding in an untouched closet. One that hadn't been touched by the fire. She tucked me under her coat and left."

"Why?"

I shrugged. "She told me that since you two were so careless that you didn't deserve a child anymore."

"What?"

"Haden, Dad, explained that it was nothing that
was done by you, nothing that you could have
prevented. Nothing to due to negligence on your side.
That someone set fire to the house and blocked all the
exits."

Mom was nodding. "Please, if we'd known we
would have spared no expense in finding you. You
were only three years old! We were completely
devastated when we thought we'd lost you!" I was
shouting and I didn't mean to. Haden got up and
came to the bed. He took my hand. "You were our
first child together."

"I'd like to get to know you now."

She started to cry. "I'm so happy that you're
here! I've missed you so much. You were my little
Benny boy!"

Suddenly I wrapped my arms around her
shoulders and hugged her. That's when Mom blacked
out.

Ben Delta   Marie Garcia

Also enjoy these other novels from Marie Garcia

Delta Files

The Hotel Slayings

The Masked Killer

Ballerina

Recreational Murder

Fake

Trea-Bella Donna

Vacay

Trea-Bella Donna: Prison Queen

Suicide Killer

State Route

Coroner

Addyson

Broken

Redemption

Addyson Private Investigations

Kaula Dawkins

Adam Corning

Pami Simpson

Ben Delta   *Marie Garcia*

Tabitha Johnson

Poetry Collections
Bored and Bleeding
Egotistical Mama
Powerful Desire
From Me to You
Blood Speaks
Remembrance
Sinking Freely
Weeping Summer
Coast to Coast
Random Designs

Short Story Collections
The Scorned American
A Perfectly Secret Affair
The Haunted Third Shift
Lonely Nights and Crimson Lips
Worlds Apart and Then Some
Second Sapphire
Deadly

Ben Delta   Marie Garcia

Key Moments

Stranded Feelings

2 in 1 Novels

Espionage Garden

Hotels Unmasked

Recreational Ballet

A Marvelous Black Death

Vacant Queen

Killer State

The Duo

The Ending

For Better or Worse

Specialty Novels

2030

Writing Death

Black Widow

Marvelous

Sai

Gypsy Rose

Ben Delta   Marie Garcia

Other Novels

Dew

Weird

Twelve Months

Better Days

Espionage: An American Tale

The Garden

Dreamland Theater

Almost Amish

Come Travel with Me

Black Widow

A Far Worse Place (Vol. 1)

Wastelands

A Better Worse Place (Vol. 2)

The Expectant Mother

The Photography Sessions

The Evil Ones

About the Author

Marie was born in Modesto, California in September of 1981 and raised in Vancouver, Washington. She graduated high school from Prairie High School in Brush Prairie, Washington in June of 2000. In January of 2006 she graduated college from Everest College (formerly Western Business College) in Vancouver, Washington.

She was raised by her maternal grandparents and has five half sisters and two half brothers.

Marie married in the fall of 2010 and they reside in Pennsylvania.